A catalogue record for this book is available from
the British Library.

First edition

Published by Ladybird Books Ltd Loughborough Leicestershire UK
Ladybird Books Inc Auburn Maine 04210 USA
© Darrell Waters Limited 1949
First published in *The Dear Old Snowman* by Brockhampton Press 1949
Enid Blyton's signature is a Registered Trade Mark of Darrell Waters Limited
© LADYBIRD BOOKS LTD MCMXCII

Printed in England (3)

Enid Blyton

Mrs Furrymouse and the Pepper Pot

illustrations by PETER STEVENSON

Ladybird Books

Two families of mice lived in the old kitchen. One was Mrs Whiskers' family and the other was Mrs Furrymouse's.

Sometimes the mice used to visit one another when the kitchen cat was not about.

When Mrs Whiskers' youngest son, Paddy-Paws, had a party, all Mrs Furrymouse's children were invited.

On the morning of the party, there was such excitement. And you should have seen the way that Mrs Furrymouse dressed her children! The boys had red trousers and blue jackets, the girls had tiny blue skirts and little shawls. They really did look smart.

When each mouse had wrapped a little present for Paddy-Paws, they were ready to go.

M rs Furrymouse first of all put her nose out of her hole to make quite sure that the cat wasn't in the kitchen. She sniffed. She could smell no cat. But she could smell cheese up on the table! A meal was laid out for the farmer.

Mrs Furrymouse made up her mind that she would have a look at that cheese when the party was over.

She set off across the kitchen with her little family.

The party was great fun. There were sausages, bacon-rind sandwiches, potato-peel pies, cheese and cakes. After the meal they all played games, and they squeaked and squealed so loudly that they didn't hear the big kitchen cat come stealing into the kitchen.

But he heard their squeaks and squeals! He blinked his big green eyes and sat himself down in a dark corner to wait until the mouse family came by.

When the party was over,
Mrs Furrymouse and her children
came quietly out of Mrs Whiskers' hole.

"We'll just go up onto the table and see
if we can nibble a bit of cheese,"
whispered Mrs Furrymouse. "Come
along! We can climb up the tablecloth.
It nearly touches the ground at the
corners."

So they all ran to the table and
scampered up the tablecloth!

The cat was cross. He had hoped that
they were going straight to their hole.
Then he could have caught them.

Now as the mice were climbing up to the table, Mrs Furrymouse caught a smell of CAT. She was frightened at once.

"Oh dear – where could the cat be?" She stood on the table and sniffed and sniffed.

"The cat is somewhere about!" she whispered to her four children. "Keep up here with me. Don't move! Oh, if only I knew whether he is over there – or by the sink – or sitting just by our own hole! It's so dark that I can't see a thing."

The five mice sat as still as could be. So did the cat. They were all listening for one another. But nobody made a sound. Not one single sound.

So the cat didn't know where the mice were and the mice didn't know where the cat was.

"**D**o we have to stay here all night?"
whispered one of the little mice.
"Why, when daylight comes, we shall be
seen!"

"Oh dear, if only I knew where that cat
is!" thought Mrs Furrymouse. "How
can I find out?"

S he ran a few steps over the tablecloth and bumped into something hard. It was the pepper pot. And that gave Mrs Furrymouse an idea! She scuttled back to her little family.

"Get out your hankies and bury your noses in them," she whispered. "I am going to shake the pepper pot as hard as I can, all round the edge of the table. Then if the cat is anywhere near, he will sneeze loudly when the pepper gets up his nose. But *you* mustn't sneeze and give away where we are – so get out your hankies!"

All the little mice got out their hankies and put their little pink noses into them.

Mrs Furrymouse picked up the pepper pot and ran to the edge of the table with it.

Shake-shake-shake! She emptied half the pepper onto the floor. Then she went to the other side. Shake-shake-shake! Down went some more yellow pepper, flying through the air. Shake-shake-shake! Shake-shake-shake!

And then a most tremendous SNEEZE came up from the floor! The cat had got some pepper up his nose and he just could *not* stop himself from sneezing!

TISHOO!
A-TISHOO!

Mrs Furrymouse scampered back to her children. "The cat is over by the sink!" she whispered. "Come along, slip down this side of the table, and run for our hole!"

Down they all went and scampered across the kitchen floor as fast as they could go.

The cat heard them, but all he could do was give another enormous sneeze that nearly shook his head off!

"A-TISHOO!" he went, just as the last mouse squeezed safely down the hole.

"Hurrah for the pepper pot!" cried Mrs Furrymouse.

And "Three cheers for Mummy Furrymouse!" cried all the little mice.